Dragon Knights ⁓
The Novellas 1

The Dragon Healer

BIANCA D'ARC

This book is a work of fiction. The names, characters, places, and incidents are products of the writer's imagination or have been used fictitiously and are not to be construed as real. Any resemblance to persons, living or dead, actual events, locale or organizations is entirely coincidental.

No part of this book may be used or reproduced in any manner whatsoever without written permission, except in the case of brief quotations embodied in critical articles and reviews.

Copyright © 2017 Bianca D'Arc
All rights reserved.
ISBN: 1979293457
ISBN-13: 978-1979293457

What's better than a knight sweeping you off your feet? Two knights.

Silla is a healer riding circuit on the border, helping those in need. When she hears the pained cries of a dragon in distress, she comes to his aid, using most of her precious supplies to help the badly injured creature.

The dragon's knight, Brodie, is fascinated by the woman—the miracle worker—who has come to help his friend. She is both beautiful and kind hearted and he quickly realizes she is his destined mate. And if she is Brodie's mate, she is Geoff's as well, for Brodie's dragon was mated to Geoff's dragon many years ago.

Geoff doesn't believe in the tales of love at first sight among knights, but he knows that when either he or Brodie finds a wife, they will share her. Hearing about the dragon's injury, Geoff and his dragon race to help, only to find the dragon on the mend and Brodie in bed with the most stunning woman Geoff has ever seen.

Love at first sight turns out to be real and it strikes them as they come together and realize that no matter what the obstacles, they are meant to be together. Silla is the missing link that will join their lives and make them a true Lair family—if they can just convince her.

Note: Knights like to get frisky and these two are no exception. Beware the passion, playfulness, a bit of bondage and a whole lot of three-way loving with a tiny bit of exhibitionism thrown in for good measure.

DEDICATION

This novella was conceived for the re-launch of my Dragon Knights series in 2013. Little did I know that the publisher would go out of business just four years later. As a result, this story, along with the first 10 books in the series are now in their 2nd editions, having been re-released under a different publisher.

I'm grateful for all the fans who have stuck with the series since its debut all those years ago. If you're new here, welcome! I hope you enjoy your visit to Draconia and the surrounding lands. I have just a few more stories to tell in this series before I bring it to a conclusion. I hope you'll all stick with me for the rest of our journey.

And the original dedication for this story stands:
This one is for the readers who have

stood by me for so long, always asking for more dragons! I'm truly honored each and every time someone comes up to me at a conference or writes to me about my books. I couldn't continue to write these stories of my heart without you. Thank you all!

And as always, I dedicate my work to my family, who supported me through several career changes. This last one was a doozy, but they never lost faith in me. I love you, guys!

CHAPTER ONE

Silla was a healer. Not the magical kind from fairy stories, but an accomplished apothecary who had trained at the High Temple of Our Lady of Light for many years before being sent out on her journeyman adventure. All healers of the Temple were sent out among the people of various lands for years at a time, to apply their skills in a real world setting. Only after a decade—or sometimes more—as a journeyman would they be invited to return to the Temple and awarded the title of Master.

Silla had at least five more years to go as a journeyman, but she didn't mind. She quite enjoyed traveling the countryside of Draconia, even if she had been given a route on the border with Skithdron. That nation had been causing more trouble of late, and Silla had seen far too many venom burns on people who had been attacked by skiths. Those evil creatures, born of magic during the Wizard Wars centuries ago, were hunters who didn't discriminate in their prey. Anything that moved was in danger around a skith.

They were huge and snake-like, with gaping maws that spit acidic venom. If the venom didn't get you, their multiple rows of serrated teeth would, snapping your head off in one fast chomp.

Luckily, skiths mostly stayed to their side of the border. The flat, rocky terrain in Skithdron was more favorable to their kind. The green, forested mountains of the Draconian border seldom saw a skith incursion—unless they were deliberately herded in that direction. It had been done during the Wizard Wars and a few times since then, but Silla had not been here then.

This new incursion was bad enough that the Draconian King had ordered the creation of a new Lair where fighting dragons and knights would live, train and protect the border. It seemed the skiths' only natural enemies were dragons. Those magical, flying creatures who could breathe fire could also—she had heard—fry a skith in its tracks. It wasn't easy, but they could do it.

Bayberry Heath was one of the small towns on Silla's route. It lay in a protected valley that was as idyllic as it was serene. The town flourished and had a lovely inn as well as several other businesses and shops. Silla always looked forward to the part of her circuit that would bring her to Bayberry Heath, and as she crested the final hill and looked down at the fertile valley, she felt a sense of joy that seldom came to her.

"See that, Hero?" She talked to her horse as if he could actually understand what she said. "We'll sleep well tonight. A bed at the inn for me and a nice stall full of fresh hay for you."

The horse snorted and plodded onward. Perhaps she only imagined that he stepped up his pace when he saw the village in the distance...or perhaps not. She'd come to respect animals and their senses much more since she'd been on the road. The animals of the forest always knew when danger was near or a storm was imminent. By learning to read their signs, she had learned how to protect herself as well.

Her horse, Hero, was old but sturdy, and they'd made a good partnership these past few years. Of course, the Temple had sent her out with little more than the clothes on her back. Part of being a journeyman was learning how to be resourceful. She had earned Hero by healing a wealthy man's wife after a dangerous childbirth. Both the child and the mother had thrived under her care and the man had been so grateful, he'd given her the horse in payment. Silla had wanted to turn him down, but she was frankly tired of all that walking between her assigned villages and farms.

A few months later, another grateful town had given her the cart after she diagnosed the reason behind an outbreak of stomach sickness. The local well had been infested with a particular kind of snail that polluted the water in such a way as to make it seem fine, but sent everyone running for the privy a few hours after drinking. Such a thing could kill the old and the young, but luckily the levels of pollution hadn't reached that critical stage before she had discovered the problem.

Again, she had tried to refuse the cart, but with it, she could make her rounds much faster. That argument, made by one of the villagers, had finally won her over. The headman of the village had spent a few days teaching Hero and Silla how to handle the cart and then they were off to the next village on their rounds.

Silla had soon discovered that the cart made an excellent bed for those nights when she could not find better shelter. She traded for some cloth in the next village and made a pallet of sorts by stuffing the sewn cloth with soft plant fibers and herbs. The herbs kept the summer bugs at bay and made a lovely, fragrant place for her to rest after a long day on the road.

The cart was more than big enough for her and her few things. A short time later, she decided she had space for other wares that she could trade in the villages for better meals and the occasional night at an inn. Silla made many kinds of medicinal potions and even potted a few rare and useful plants that she could barter or give to her patients when needed. Over the past few years, she'd built up a very nice apothecary shop from which the residents of each village could obtain herbal preparations made by an expert hand or even the plants from which they could make their own remedies, depending on the season. But she never charged for medicines or plants when her patients truly needed them. That was the creed by which her Temple lived. Still, she was able to make a few coins from those who were not ailing and traded more often than not for foodstuffs and other items that would help her do her job in more comfort.

Her route overlapped with another, more senior member of her Temple now and again. He would check on her progress in person, in addition to the written reports she sent back every season to the main Temple. Someone there kept track of the spread of illnesses based on journeymen reports and also kept an eye on the journeymen themselves. The accumulation of wealth was not encouraged. Their order was to live simply, but those who were industrious in bringing remedies to the people along their routes even before the medicines were needed were often rewarded with higher positions in the Temple when they returned to become Masters.

Silla was about halfway there now. According to the older healer she'd spent a companionable afternoon with a fortnight ago, she was progressing well. Another five years or so, and she'd be able to return to the

Temple with her head held high.

She almost regretted the fact that she'd have to go back. Silla had found that she enjoyed the freedom to travel where she willed. Actually being at the Temple was much more restrictive. Of course, it was better than what her life had been before.

As dusk settled over the valley of Bayberry Heath, Silla topped the last small rise that led down into the village. The innkeeper was already lighting his lanterns to welcome strangers in the night. She could see the little dot of flame dance and bounce as he walked along the gate, lighting the two lanterns on either side of the entrance to his yard that would burn through the night to welcome weary travelers.

It was a sight for sore eyes. And this time, she didn't have to imagine Hero's pace picking up as he probably scented other horses in the stable not too far away. A few more minutes and they'd be there in time for a nice dinner of fresh fodder for Hero and good, hot food she didn't have to prepare for herself. She could almost taste the inn's savory stew. She closed her eyes for just a moment, imagining how good it was going to taste.

Suddenly, an inhuman bellow of unmistakable pain shattered the night. Silla's eyes flew open as she searched for the source of the sound. It had come from up ahead and frightened Hero into a near standstill.

She got him going again, even as she searched the night for whatever had made that tone of pure anguish. If there was any way she could help, she would, but she had no idea what kind of creature could have made such a noise. It wasn't any of the domesticated animals she knew. She'd been called upon to heal a cow or horse more than once and hadn't minded in the least. Her skills were for all things living—person, animal or plant.

Hero balked only once more as they entered the inn yard, and his reasons became clear at once. Next to the inn, on the side away from the horse stables, was an open area filled with sand that Silla had seen before but never questioned. Now she understood why it was there. It was an area set aside for dragons. There was one there now.

It was the dragon that had howled in pain as a big man poured bucket after bucket of water on what looked like deep, acidic burns around the joint where wing met body. Silla winced in sympathy as the creature writhed in pain. Smoke puffed out of his nostrils, but he seemed to be making an effort to contain his agony as the man scurried with the help of what looked to be every able-bodied person from the village.

The innkeeper saw her and came right over, grabbing on to Hero's halter.

"Thank the Mother of All you've come, Healer Silla. If ever there was a need for your medicines, it is now. Can you help yon dragon? We would all count it as a favor. He went down protecting us from a rogue skith and is badly burned."

Silla jumped down from her cart and grabbed her satchel. "I will see what I can do. Will you take Hero to the stables? Leave the cart in easy reach. There are some plants in back that I may need for the dragon's treatment, if his knight will allow."

"Sure thing, mistress. And thank ye." The innkeeper took charge of her horse and cart while Silla approached the dragon and all the people trying to help him.

Sir Broderick was at his wit's end, trying

to help his dragon partner, Phelan, his best friend in all the world. They had been in tight spaces before, but never had Phelan been so injured or in such pain.

They'd fought skiths before and come out unharmed. It had been a lucky—or rather, *un*lucky—shot that had taken Phelan down this time. Thankfully, the good people of Bayberry Heath had been willing to help, getting as much water as they could to bathe the wound free of the terrible acid.

Brodie didn't know what else to do. They'd poured as much water as they could on the burns, bathing the dragon thoroughly. The acid was diluted enough by now to be harmless, draining away into the sand pit beneath them. But Phelan was still in terrible pain.

The shoulder joint on a dragon was one of his few vulnerable places. The acid had eaten deep into Phelan's flesh before they'd been able to land and get water on it. Brodie felt anguish at not knowing what to do to help ease Phelan's pain.

"Sir, I am a journeyman healer from the High Temple of Our Lady of Light. Though I have never treated a dragon before, I offer what help my humble skills may bring to your partner."

The soft voice at his side distracted Brodie for a moment. He turned and stopped in his tracks. Before him was an angel sent from above, a gorgeous woman in the simple clothes of a healer. The marks of her Temple were clearly visible on her cloak, and Brodie thought he'd never seen a more beautiful sight.

"Mistress, we welcome any help you may give." Brodie found his voice after a moment of pure shock. "I confess, I don't know what else to do to ease Phelan's pain. Please help him." That last bit came out on a broken whisper, but Brodie couldn't help it. He had looked back at Phelan while speaking and realized once more he'd never seen his dragon partner in such bad shape. It hurt Brodie to see the great dragon humbled so much.

She started forward even before he'd finished speaking, urgency in her steps, though she approached the dragon carefully. Brodie caught up with her and escorted her to Phelan's worst injury, that in the bend where wing met body.

The healer had pulled a jar from her satchel and uncapped it. Brodie could smell the scent of healing herbs, and he knew the jar contained something that would halt Phelan's pain. That ointment would numb anywhere it touched. Brodie had seen and felt its effects before. This woman could help Phelan. Brodie was sure of it.

Rather than slather on the medicine right away, the healer took a moment to examine Phelan's injury with sure hands. She even bent to smell the wound and used a clean cloth from her pack to dry the area around it as best she could from the dousing the villagers had helped Brodie accomplish.

The moment she applied the ointment, Phelan began to breathe easier. As did Brodie.

"This cream has an anesthetic in it, so the pain should ease," the healer said in a gentle voice.

"Whatever you are doing, keep doing it," came Phelan's voice, filled with relief, in Brodie's mind.

"It's working," Brodie reported to the healer. "He says to keep going."

She continued to work, talking quietly as she ministered to the dragon. "So you really speak to your dragon partner. I had heard tales, but I have never seen a dragon up close before, much less talked to a knight. I have wondered how such different beings managed to work together so well."

"Only men who can hear the silent speech of dragons are eligible to be chosen as knights," he answered offhandedly, watching her treatment of his best friend carefully.

"I see." She examined the wound more closely now that the pain had been masked. "This burn is severe, but I believe we can make him more comfortable while it heals." She turned to address the innkeeper who had returned without Brodie realizing it. "Can you get six burnjelly plants from my cart, please? The biggest ones," she clarified.

The innkeeper scurried off to do her bidding. Brodie recognized the name of an uncommon plant that was highly prized for its ability to heal burns. In the southern part of the country, he knew many housewives and innkeepers liked to keep a burnjelly plant potted and growing on a sunny windowsill if they could get their hands on one. It was a rare thing and something of a miracle that this healer had a supply in the back of her wagon.

She hummed softly while she worked and

the sound seemed to calm Phelan. It calmed Brodie too, if truth be told. Between the humming and the confident way she worked to clean and inspect all of his dragon partner's wounds, Brodie felt he was in good hands. Thanks be to the Mother of All.

Phelan had fallen into a light doze, Brodie realized. The prolonged battle, the injury and the pain had wiped him out. The cessation of the worst of his agony had probably allowed the dragon to shut down for a little while and recover some of his strength. Phelan, Brodie had learned over the years they'd been together, had cultivated the ability to take what he called *battle naps*.

He could deliberately sleep, at will, for short amounts of time that would allow him to stay on duty much longer than most of the other dragons. Phelan had developed the skill while he'd been recovering from the loss of his first knight. Phelan was a dragon in the prime of his life, and even though partnering with a dragon extended the knight's lifetime two or three times over, eventually they still died. When the knight died, the dragon usually went into a period of deep mourning.

Phelan's first knight, Sir Anarik, had died

in battle after only a hundred years or so together. He had been one of those defending the old king and his wife when they had been murdered. Phelan and Sir Anarik had gone after the assassins and Anarik had died, leaving Phelan riderless and heartbroken.

Rather than sink into deeper despair, Phelan had set himself the task of safeguarding the remainder of the royal family, in particular the princes, the eldest of whom had become king on his father's death. Roland had been very young when he took the throne, but he had done a masterful job. Attempts had been made on his and his brothers' lives, but Phelan had usually be there to skewer or fry any who tried to kill any more of the royal family.

Which is why Phelan had learned to do without much sleep while on duty. He and another partnerless dragon had devised the scheme and shared the duty of guarding the princes all on their own. They hadn't told anyone, but after they'd conveniently defeated a few would-be assassins, people began to realize what the dragons had done.

King Roland had elevated Phelan, thanking him for his tireless service by making him a member of the Dragon Council and one of the king's most trusted advisors on military matters. When the time had come to build the Border Lair, Phelan had been on top of the list of seasoned warriors who could put the place together.

Brodie had the military and engineering experience to handle such a task. Even before he'd been chosen by Phelan, he'd had the beginnings of a successful career with the specialized group of Guardsmen who assessed the safety of bridges and other public structures. He'd studied building and architecture in some detail as a young man and put that, along with his penchant for warfare, to good use as a military engineer.

His partnership with Phelan had come along quite by accident. A river had spilled violently over its banks, taking out a key bridge during a particularly bad storm. Brodie had been sent to repair the bridge. Phelan had been there to help with the rescue, plucking people and livestock out of the raging torrent and flying them to shore. When Phelan realized Brodie was one of the rare men who could hear him speak, they began to work together to help during the crisis.

After the emergency was over, Phelan hadn't wasted much time in speaking the words of Claim to Brodie and they had been partners ever since. Brodie moved from Guard post to Lair and had begun training in the ways of knights. His earlier fighting experience came in more than handy and his logical mind helped him move up the ranks in record time. He was a strategist and highly trained engineer, which was something the king could well use in his ranks of Dragon Knights and top advisors.

The only thing preventing Phelan from being appointed leader of the new Lair was his knight's lack of a mate. Mated pairs were considered more stable for leading Lairs, so Phelan and by extension, Brodie, were given the role of seconds-in-command of the new Lair.

The innkeeper returned rolling a wheelbarrow filled with potted plants. Sure enough, Brodie recognized the distinctive, puffy stalks of the burnjelly plant from his travels in the south. He took one of the plants as the healer did the same and began snapping off some of the outer stalks and preparing the jelly inside for use.

"You've done this before?" the healer

asked in her quiet way.

"I have seen it done," Brodie confirmed. "I can help. I realize you're going to need to use a lot of your supply on Phelan, but I can pay you."

"When there is need, there is no charge," the healer repeated the oft-heard motto of her Temple. Still, Brodie knew many healers made small amounts of money selling medicines in the towns they visited. It was never much, but it probably provided for the occasional creature comfort.

"A noble sentiment. Nevertheless, I will compensate you for the plants. I know how rare they are in these climes."

"I'll let you in on a little secret," she whispered with a mischievous expression, leaning toward him.

She smelled of lavender and lilies and warm woman. A heady combination that made him want to lean closer and breathe deeply. She was a gorgeous creature and now that Phelan was resting more comfortably, Brodie saw again what he'd seen when he first beheld her. This healer was a beauty with a gentle touch and an attractive scent. He wanted to kiss her, but he knew that would be entirely inappropriate at the moment. Still, if the opportunity presented itself later, he wouldn't be shy. He wanted to see if she tasted as sweet as she smelled.

"If we only use the outer stalks," she went on, oblivious to his carnal thoughts, "the plant will survive to grow more in time. Even trimmed as these will be when we are done, I can earn a few pennies with them from the villagers to pay for my room and board." She smiled and leaned back, snapping another of the outer stalks off her plant and cutting it open. "So you see, I will not be out much from helping your friend. To be honest, I am honored to assist a dragon and knight of the realm."

"You honor us with your skill and willingness to help, healer," Brodie replied politely. "I'm Sir Broderick, but my friends call me Brodie. What's your name?"

"Silla," she replied softly, almost shyly.

He wondered how a lovely, attractive and obviously skilled woman had ended up in such a lonely occupation, but he would not pry. Not yet. Soon though, he vowed to know all her secrets.

"You are lovely, Silla." Brodie wondered where the restraint he usually practiced in his words had suddenly gone. He hadn't meant to blurt out his thoughts like that, but she seemed to be blushing in the dim light of the torch-lit courtyard.

No coy court games for this beauty. No, she was more genuine and unpracticed in her responses. Shy. Beautiful, soft-spoken and shy. Brodie never would have expected it of an obviously successful journeyman healer. To be on the road by one's self took a strong character and usually meant the traveling healers were much surer of themselves and somehow…brasher. But this woman could still blush.

Brodie found himself enchanted by the puzzle of her.

CHAPTER TWO

Silla was flattered and somewhat uncomfortable with the knight's attention. She didn't know how to reply to his words. Few men had ever made such dramatic statements to her. Most saw her as a healer first, woman second. If at all.

She busied herself with preparing the plant stalks she would need to treat the dragon. Reaching into her satchel, she retrieved one of a set of small bowls she often used to mix herbs. It would do as a vessel to hold the jelly as she worked. She began scraping the jelly out of the cut stalks into the bowl. The knight followed suit, bending close to her as she worked.

He was so tall. And younger than she was, if she didn't miss her guess. His dark curls made her fingers itch to touch them and see if they were as soft as they looked.

He had brown hair kissed with streaks of gold, cut short in the warrior fashion, but curly in the most attractive way. It was windblown from his flight here, no doubt, and soot covered his clothes and made a stripe across one cheek.

He smiled at her, a question in his eyes. "Is there something on my face?"

Drat. She'd been caught staring.

"Yes." She was forced to explain her fascination with his handsome features. "Soot, I believe," she answered quietly.

"A hazard of working with dragons." He chuckled and surprised her by leaning closer, offering his cheek. "Could you?" he asked with seeming innocence, but he had a devilish smile on his face.

Silla decided to take up his challenge. Daring greatly, she took a clean cloth from her satchel and wiped at the gray mark along his cheek. The rasp of his beard stubble made her insides quiver and she damned the layer of cloth between her fingers and his skin. She wanted to feel the heat of his body, the bristles on his cheek.

It was irrational. She hadn't ever wanted another man since the dissolution of her disastrous marriage. She thought she'd been forever cured of the yearnings she'd once known as a younger woman. Yearnings that had been demolished and replaced by the repulsion she'd learned in her painful marriage bed.

But this knight...he was different. He made her feel things she hadn't dreamed of in too many years to count. He reawakened something in her that wanted to know more. Other women seemed to enjoy bedding their mates. Many talked to her, in the course of her duties as a healer, about the intimacies of the bedroom. She'd come to realize that not all husbands were oafish brutes. Some were tender and loving with their wives. Some lovers were also overly playful and got into mischief that required her services to heal.

She knew all this with an academic sort of viewpoint, but she'd never imagined she would want to know the touch of a man again. Not until meeting this amazing, alarming, disarming knight.

The soot on his cheek was long gone, but the moment held. Their gazes locked and his head dipped lower, closer to hers.

A clang out in the yard made her jump and the moment was broken. She looked over to see the innkeeper ushering the last of the townsfolk into his common room. There were many who had joined in the bucket brigade to help the dragon. They were all now enjoying a drink. She had heard Brodie—Sir Broderick, she reminded herself sternly—make the offer of a round of drinks on him by way of thanks as the last of the buckets was emptied.

Silla looked down at her hands and saw there was enough jelly in the bowl to at least begin treating the dragon's burns. The sooner they got the jelly on the wound, the sooner the burns would start to heal.

She moved away from the disturbing knight and closer, once again, to the dragon.

"There is another bowl like this one, in the first pocket of my satchel," she said without meeting Brodie's eyes. Blast! She had to remember to think of him as Sir Broderick. Brodie was much too familiar for a knight of the realm. "If you could continue preparing the jelly, sir, I will begin treatment."

She heard a sigh and then movement behind her as the knight reached into her pack, which was lying on the ground. She observed him finding the second bowl out of the corner of her eye as she scooped a handful of the jelly out of her bowl and began dabbing it gently on the dragon's wounds.

She began to hum a healing chant as she worked, using light strokes on the dragon's raw flesh, making certain every last inch of the damaged areas were covered. She ran out of jelly quickly, but Brodie—Sir Broderick—proved an excellent assistant, handing her a full bowl when hers emptied. They repeated the dance quite a few times before all the dragon's burns were treated.

When she turned back to the area he'd been working in, she found all her potted plants well pruned with the growing centers intact. The plants would live to grow new stalks. He had been listening. She smiled in satisfaction. A man who really listened was a rare and wondrous thing in her experience.

"That should do for now." She rubbed the excess burnjelly off her hands with a small square of cloth. "We should leave the wounds open to the air tonight. Do you think he can sleep in this position? If he rolls and gets dirt in the open wounds, it would be bad." She looked over at the dragon's head, surprised to find his eyes open and his head turned to look at her. "Well, hello there, Sir Dragon. I hope you are feeling better than when you came in." She bowed low, holding the dragon's gaze. Everyone who was sent into Draconia by the Temple was given instruction on how to deal with dragons should they cross paths with one. There was a certain etiquette to be followed.

"I feel much better. Thank you, healer. I will sleep now and not move from this position. I am comfortable enough."

The great head turned and settled on the dragon's front leg, his eyes closing. Silla was still shocked immobile by the sound of the dragon's booming voice inside her head. Never had she imagined such a thing, but there could be no doubt. It was the dragon who had spoken to her, silently, in her mind.

Silla shook her head as she gathered her supplies and put them in the wheelbarrow with the now much smaller plants. She passed the knight as she did so, knowing she had many chores to see to before she could rest this night.

"Your companion will require further treatments," Silla told the man. "I will prepare the jelly tonight and apply it at first light, if that is all right with you, sir." She kept busy while she talked to him, mentally taking stock of what she needed to do before going to sleep and the subsequent dawn.

A hand on her forearm stopped her when she would have lifted the handles of the wheelbarrow. She looked up to meet the gaze of Sir Broderick. Brodie.

She was caught in his gaze. He was closer than she had imagined. Closer and far handsomer than any man had a right to be. She felt breathless again at his proximity.

"Allow me," he said in a quiet voice as he lifted the wheelbarrow and waited. It struck her that he was waiting for her to direct him.

"You're very kind, sir." She knew she was blushing as she led the way toward where her cart was parked next to the stables. There was a water pump nearby and an empty trough that would serve her purposes. She had to clean the implements of her trade and prepare them for tomorrow before she could seek her bed.

*

Much to her surprise, Sir Broderick did not leave after delivering the laden wheelbarrow. He had placed it alongside her cart so she could move the now-bare plants into the covered storage area with the rest of her stock. At the same time, she removed four plants that still had all their stalks and put them into the wheelbarrow with the two empty bowls they had used before, plus two more bowls she retrieved from the back of her cart.

Brodie—make that Sir Broderick—stayed by her side and picked up the wheelbarrow once again when she moved toward the empty trough. She got there first and began pumping water into the basin. She didn't need much. Just enough to wash her implements and her hands.

She realized then that Sir Broderick's hands were probably still covered in the slimy jelly.

"If you want to wash your hands first, I'll pump the water for you," she offered.

He looked like he wanted to argue the point, but gave in after a moment's consideration. "I would be much obliged."

Brodie—no, she must think of him as Sir Broderick, lest she slip and become far too familiar—moved close, washing his hands briskly. He was so large, and so near. He had been through battle, injury and his dragon's pain today and he still seemed so strong and vital. Because the pump was small and the space limited, she couldn't help but stand very close indeed to his tall, muscular form. Even in the flickering light from the lanterns all around the inn's yard, she could clearly see the masculine lines of his angular jaw, straight nose and strong chin. He was really too handsome for his own good. For her good too.

She tried to avert her gaze downward, but that brought her focus to his thickly muscled arms, rippling as he moved. She lowered her gaze even more and was caught by the sight of his strong thighs, encased in black leather that followed his form so faithfully. Her mouth went dry at the sight.

Then she noticed the tear in the soft hide of his pants. And the blood.

"You're injured," she whispered, shocked he hadn't been limping or even once complained of the discomfort he must be in. She could readily see the angry red gash along his right thigh. It looked deep and very painful. She had seen such wounds before. She knew what they did to a normal man. That this brave knight was still standing and acting as if nothing was wrong, was a testament to his fortitude.

"It's just a scratch," he replied, glancing down at his thigh and shaking his head. His nonchalant attitude amazed her.

"That is more than a scratch, my lord." Normally she would not have argued the point, but perhaps, she admitted within her restless mind, she wanted to prolong this encounter. She didn't want to leave his presence yet. His wound was a fantastic excuse for her to spend just a few more minutes with him.

"I will wash it when I get to my room." He shrugged, as if it were of little importance. "Let me help you get set for the morning first. I want to help in whatever way I can, since you are being so kind and generous aiding Phelan."

"It is my honor and my duty, milord," she replied, slightly embarrassed by his praise. "But if it will get you off that leg faster, by all means, let us get down to business. This will not take long. And then I insist on dressing your leg wound. It will not help your dragon if you fall from an infection that could have been easily avoided."

He smiled then and her breathing faltered. He was potent at close range. He was incredibly handsome—why couldn't she stop thinking that?—and seemingly unaware of his effect on a female's ability to think clearly in his presence. With slightly addled wits, she changed places with him and allowed him to operate the water pump. She cleaned her tools and her hands as quickly as possible, wringing out the small cloths she had used that were not that soiled. She would let them dry overnight. The cloths that were truly dirty, she segregated into a small pile for later attention.

For the next ten minutes, they worked companionably, cutting the outer stalks off the new batch of plants and preparing the jelly for tomorrow morning. Burnjelly was more potent when it had between twelve and twenty-four hours to set before use. This batch would be even more helpful to the dragon in the morning as long as they were careful to cover it securely overnight.

They sat on the edge of the half-empty trough, each working silently at first. They worked well together, establishing a rhythm. Brodie—Sir Broderick—was good company and did not balk at work, even while injured. She was more impressed by him the more she was around him.

"So tell me, how did you come to the Temple?" Brodie asked out of the blue after they had been working for a few minutes.

She was so surprised by his question, she almost dropped her knife into the trough. Regaining her balance, and her equilibrium somewhat, she thought about how to answer his question. It was a loaded one, to be sure.

CHAPTER THREE

"It is a long story and a sad one for the most part," she said finally, deciding to give him a little bit of the truth. "I was married off young to an old man. When he wanted to be rid of me, he beat me and threw me out into the street. A kind-hearted soul called one of the brothers from our order and he treated me. It was a long recovery and over the time I spent in the Temple gardens, I discovered an affinity for plants. They allowed me to stay on and join the order to train has an apothecary. As you can see, I made it through to journeyman." She shrugged, gesturing toward her cart.

"How long have you been on the road?" He seemed to understand more about the way the Temple worked than most people.

"About five years. I'm almost halfway through my journeyman trial."

"You have done very well for yourself." He gave an approving glance to the cart and her stock of rare plants.

"You seem much more familiar with the Temple and its ways than most people I come across. How is it you know so much about the order?"

"We knights meet many people on our journeys, but as it happens, someone dear to me is a member of your order."

"Truly? Do you think I would know him?"

Sir Broderick gave her a secretive smile. "Oh, I would bet you know him if you spent any time at all in the Temple gardens. Have you met Brother Osric?"

"Osric? He is the best of us. The leader of all apothecaries in our order."

"He is my brother," Brodie said in a playful voice, as if sharing some private joke, but she didn't quite understand. It was becoming increasingly difficult to think of him as *Sir* Broderick when he was so open and warm. The shortened version of his name fit his friendly manner, and she knew it was a losing battle to keep that more formal distance between them in her mind.

"That's not possible. He is probably old

enough to be your father," she said with a scowl of confusion.

"A benefit of joining my life to a dragon's." Sir—make that Brodie—glanced toward the sandy area where the dragon lay sleeping. "I will outlive my baby brother, Osric, by many years. Perhaps a lifetime or two." He shrugged, but she saw the discomfort of that knowledge sitting restlessly in his eyes, even in the flickering lantern light. "I was chosen by Phelan when I was the age you probably are guessing me to be. In truth, I've lived double that time already, even though my body stays as youthful as it was when Phelan gave me just a tiny portion of his magic."

"I have never heard of such a thing," she admitted, allowing some of the awe she felt to be heard in her tone.

"It is not widely known, though it isn't a secret, exactly. So few men can be knights, it isn't something that regular folk seem to concern themselves with."

"So you're really older than me, though you look younger," she thought out loud. Only after she realized what she had said did the blush start in her cheeks.

He sent her a speculative glance. "Indeed,

mistress. I am far older and wiser than a pretty young thing like you." He chuckled, leaning forward to place the plant he'd been working on in the nearby wheelbarrow. The action brought him closer to her and for a heart-stopping moment, she thought perhaps he meant to kiss her.

The disappointment she felt when he didn't was involuntary, but all too real. She'd only just met the man and already, she wanted to feel his kiss.

She wanted even more than that, if truth be told.

"Living so long must be a blessing indeed," she said, speaking quickly to cover her confusion. She hadn't really thought through her words and the way he looked at her made her realize their folly. It was not a gift to watch one's family grow old and die. "Forgive me," she added, looking down at her work, embarrassed yet again by her reactions to this confusing knight.

The back of his fingers touched her cheek, then her jaw, so gently. It was like a butterfly's caress. A strong butterfly that urged her to look up and meet his gaze. She complied, feeling much like a young girl, quivering at such an innocent caress.

"I can never regret joining my life to Phelan's. He is my best friend," he said simply. "But all knights search for a family of their own. We know we will eventually lose the family we were born to when we are chosen. It seems a small price when you consider the amazing benefits of partnering with a dragon and being able to train and fight to protect our land and our people. It was my life's ambition to become a knight and I was never happier than the day Phelan first spoke the words of Claim upon me." He withdrew his hand from her face, but held his gaze. "But I will always search for the woman who can complete our circle."

That sounded serious. And why was he looking at her so speculatively all of a sudden? Could he possibly think she was the woman he seemed so determined to find? She felt breathless once more, but then she recalled the strange things she had heard about marriage in dragon Lairs.

She stood and shook a bit of dirt that had fallen from one of the plant pots off her skirt. It was as good an excuse as any to put some distance between herself and this confusing man.

"And by circle, what exactly do you

mean?" She walked over to her cart for something to do, pretending to need something out of the back.

She was unprepared to feel his hard warmth at her back, his hands on her shoulders. She was up against the wheel of the cart, reaching over the waist-high side when he trapped her with nothing more than his heat and his light touch on her neck. Just one finger. Stroking. Raising goose flesh with the slow, back-and-forth motion against the sensitive skin just under her ear.

"Phelan is an older dragon," he said, confusing her yet again. Although it was probably his touch that made every last brain cell she owned jump around in mixed delight and panic. "He has a mate. She is named Qwila and her knight is called Geoff. He was chosen only about a decade ago and is probably about your age, maybe a bit older, if that makes any difference to you." That tantalizing finger moved to trace her ear and her insides quivered while her body shivered. "When one of us finds the woman who can complete our circle, only then will Phelan and Qwila be able to join once more in a mating flight. Until we have a woman of our own, Phelan and Qwila must abstain. Don't you feel sorry for them?"

He chuckled lightly and she felt the soft whisper of his breath against her ear, increasing her shivering.

"I guess so," she answered, not really understanding what she was responding to. She'd lost the thread of his conversation somewhere along the line. His touch was too distracting. Too arousing. Too amazing.

He moved away slightly, both hands dropping to her shoulders. With gentle urging, he turned her to face him, her back against the side of the cart.

His head dipped lower. Slowly. So slow, she could easily have objected, but she found herself powerless in the face of his advancing ardor. She wanted his kiss. Now, more than ever, as he'd worked her into a small frenzy of need with that simple, stirring touch.

His mouth met hers and she slipped happily under the waves of his desire, awash in sensation she had never felt before. Not once in her life had she felt so aroused by a kiss.

Her opinion of sex was undergoing a startling revision as Brodie taught her about passion. Flaming, brutal, enslaving passion. All with a simple kiss. His hands remained on her shoulders, only his mouth claiming hers, taking possession.

His taste was divine. Hot. Carnal. Manly. He was temptation itself, daring her to go farther, to follow him into the flames of perdition. Silla was lost. Brodie was her anchor in a whirlwind of chaotic pleasure. Her guide and her teacher. Her salvation.

When the kiss ended, it wasn't because she drew away. No, Brodie had stepped back, and belatedly Silla heard the loud bang of a metal bucket inside the stable, not far from them. The stable boy, no doubt, was seeing to his charges and the noise had probably reminded Brodie they were not necessarily alone.

Silla was grateful he'd stopped before anyone saw more than what had been, after all, just a kiss. She had a reputation to uphold in this town. She had to be circumspect in all her dealings with men, lest they get the wrong idea about her. Respect was important to a healer's success. If the people you treated had no respect for you, they would seldom listen to your advice. It had taken a long time to prove her worth as a healer to the people along her circuit and she didn't want to ruin that hard work with idle gossip about her willingness to succumb to a handsome young man.

"Sir Phelan should be good for tonight. He said he wouldn't move out of position, which will help the wound heal more cleanly."

"Wait. You could hear him?" Brodie stopped in his tracks, but she wasn't going to be waylaid. She wanted to get inside, away from temptation.

"Well, of course. It was a first for me, to be sure, but he talks to you every day, doesn't he?" She didn't wait for an answer, not looking at him as she gathered her things.

Moving briskly, she turned away from Brodie and bustled around the wheelbarrow. She put the bundle of dirty laundry into her cart along with the now much-smaller plants. The oilskin cover she used to keep the back of her cart dry in rainy weather went over the top, securing everything for the night. The delicate plants would keep well under the cover if the temperature dipped too low for them.

She couldn't look at Brodie as she finished her preparations for the morrow, but she felt his silent presence there.

Watching her. Probably waiting for some sign or trying to figure her out. She wished him luck with that. She couldn't even understand her own motivations or responses at this point. Sir Broderick and his devastating kiss had her in a dizzying storm of confusion.

But what lovely confusion it was.

Dare she turn to him and let the passion he inspired consume her? Silla had trod a safe and narrow path for so long, she wasn't sure if she still had it in her to be daring.

"I take my leave of you, Sir Broderick," she said formally, dropping a small curtsey, unable to meet his gaze.

"I will see you to the inn," he said softly, taking her arm and moving them forward, toward the wide front door of the well-lit common room. "And don't you think you should call me Brodie? If anyone in this village is entitled to such liberties, it is you, my dear." His teasing tone made her look up at him as they walked quietly across the large inn yard.

"Brodie, then," she amended, finding that little spark within that wanted her to jump headfirst into this man's arms and not look back.

His grin teased her and made her steps falter, but they continued their slow progress across the well-trod yard. She realized then her scandalous behavior. She had kissed the man as if there was no tomorrow and they had only just met. The thought made her pause. It made her wonder if she was just one in a long string of conquests for the handsome knight.

Brodie must have read something of her mood in her response because he stopped their progress and turned her to face him.

"Just to be clear, milady, I do not go around kissing every pretty lass that crosses my path. Tonight has been unique in many different ways and I am not too proud to admit that Phelan's condition has put me off balance." His deep brown eyes begged for understanding and showed just a tiny bit of the vulnerability he was feeling with his dragon partner laid low with such a grievous injury.

Silla's soft heart thawed. "I did not wish to be one of many, my lord," she answered honestly.

"My dear, you are one in a million. Exceptionally unique. Never to be duplicated." His smile lit her world for a brief moment.

She turned back to the inn, her heart filled with joy. Lantern light spilled out the windows and music could be heard wafting on the night breeze. They spoke no more as he opened the large door for her and they discovered the locals were having an impromptu party. It didn't show any signs of stopping and nobody noticed them standing in the darkened doorway. The innkeeper and his staff were being run off their feet by demands for food and drink.

Silla felt every bit of her weariness. It had been a long day on the road and then treating the dragon and meeting his knight who disturbed her peace on so many levels. She was bone-weary and didn't want to have to battle through the crowd to get the innkeeper's attention, much less have to haggle with the man for room and board.

"It is busier than I thought in here," Brodie spoke in a low voice, next to her ear. "Is your room already settled?"

She shook her head no, feeling tears threatening. Tears? She didn't know why she was so emotional. She had been walking this path now for five years. Her patients must be seen to before her own needs, but tonight she wished—as she had a few times before, in weak moments—for someone to help her. A partner. A friend. Someone to help ease her path in life as she tried to ease the way for others. Sometimes it felt like the weight of the world had settled on her shoulders and she had to hold it up for everyone else.

Sometimes—in the darkest hours of the night—she prayed for someone to help hold up that heavy weight on her shoulders. Someone to help her as she helped him.

But she knew from bitter experience that having a man in her life was no guarantee of such things. She had hoped for a good friend. Perhaps a lover. Even a pet could help ease some of her load. In fact, she had renamed her horse Hero because he was, in his own way, her hero. He had come into her life at a time when she had grown too tired and weak to walk from place to place. The healer had become sick of walking and her Hero had arrived to carry her where she needed to go, giving her time and energy to heal herself so she could continue to heal others.

"There is a special room always kept ready for patrolling knights," Brodie told her. "The entrance is on the outside, very near the sand pit so we can be near our partners. There are two beds in the room. You could share it with me," he offered.

CHAPTER FOUR

Silla turned to look up into his eyes. She saw no trickery in his bottomless brown gaze, though the firelight brought out lively flecks of gold in his otherwise pure brown irises.

"I am weary to my bones," she told him honestly. "If you expect more than to simply share the room, I will seek shelter elsewhere."

"I am a knight and a gentleman," he protested, but with a gentle smile that said he understood her caution. "You have my word I will not molest you in the night. On the contrary, I will protect you. Especially since you are the purveyor of burnjelly to heal my dearest friend in the world." He winked at her, and she caught his humor. He really did seem to be a nice man.

"Then I will take you up on your offer, relying on your discretion. My reputation is all I have and I would not lose it lightly." She looked around at the gathered villagers. Many were well on the way to intoxication and nobody seemed to notice her standing by the door.

"I understand, milady. Your honor will come to no harm from me," he promised.

She followed as Brodie led the way out the door and into the flickering light of the lantern-lit yard. They retraced their steps back toward the dragon wallow and up to a small door built into the side of the inn. Sure enough, when he opened it, there was a bedroom. Large by inn standards, it was comfortably appointed. Not too fancy, nor too plain. It was large enough for two big knights and their gear to bunk down comfortably.

One thing she did notice, though, was that one of the beds was built on the enormous side of large. The other was clearly a single bed. She put her cloak and the small pack she'd taken from her cart on that one, but Brodie seemed to notice her confusion as he sat on the much larger bed and smiled at her.

"This bed is built for married knights and their lady. The other is for when single knights patrol together. The senior of the pair gets the larger bed and the junior has to make do on that." He pointed to the small bed behind her.

"It will do well enough for me," she countered, feeling weary again. She turned away, releasing her outer robe. She caught it before it fell to the floor and draped it neatly over the chair that stood beside the smaller bed.

She felt the unnerving caress of Brodie's gaze as she took off as much of her outer garments as she dared. She would sleep in her dress. She had done so before and was used to it.

A sudden thought struck her as she sorted through her small pack. "I'm sorry. I forgot all about your leg injury. Shall we tend to it now?" She picked up the other satchel that held her emergency supplies. She never went anywhere without that well-worn bag.

"I told you, it's nothing."

"Please allow me to be the judge of that. Take off your pants and lie down."

"Now that's what I like to hear." Brodie's eyes twinkled up at her, and she had to laugh.

She took out an oilskin and towels to put

under his leg so they wouldn't soil the bed linens with his blood. She'd have to clean the wound first and for that she brought over the basin and water pitcher she found waiting on a small table by the door. The water was fresh, she noted from its smell, and the basin would suit her purposes. She poured a small amount of water into the basin and added cleansing herbs that would ensure his wound was disinfected and the pain dulled somewhat.

When she returned to the bed, he'd complied with her request. He was dressed in a simple shirt that hung past his hips. He had to have had the tunic on under his leathers, but she hadn't noticed it before. He'd shed his leather riding gear, including his jacket, boots and pants, and his long legs were bare to her inspection.

She used a small square of clean cloth, dipping it into the water that had turned a pale yellow as the dried herbs released their healing properties. In her line of work, she went through a lot of linen and had to keep her satchel full of clean cloths, bandages, towels and rags at all times. She had restocked her supply from the back of her cart without thinking, but was glad of it now.

The wound was deep and had bled quite a bit.

Silla tried not to think about the muscled legs with only a dusting of hair. She had worked on many male patients before, but none had elicited this kind of feminine response from her. She felt a little shaky as she approached him, the cloth in the basin she carried. She sat on the side of the huge bed, putting the basin at his side.

"Can you hold this steady?" she asked perfunctorily, not even waiting for him to take hold of the rim of the basin before reaching for the wet cloth. She rung it out a bit, then went immediately to work on the wound.

She tried to be as gentle as possible, but she saw the way his leg muscles clenched when she probed.

"I'm sorry, but the wound must be as clean as possible before infection can set in. I'm surprised you were walking on this for so long." She worked carefully but steadily, using a towel to catch the bloody water. "The herbs will disinfect and numb the area. It should not hurt so much in a minute, once the effect takes hold."

"It feels better already, Silla. Don't worry.

I've had worse and lived to tell the tale."

She knew the truth of that just by looking at the collection of scars on his legs. Some were old, some new. Many were bigger than the one he would gain from this injury. They told a story of life hard lived. A body that was used to fighting and hard work...and war.

Silla didn't comment as she continued her work. She used all the treated water before she was satisfied the wound was indeed clean enough. He'd stopped flinching early on, thanks to the anesthetic in the water, and she'd been able to get to the bottom of the cut to see that it wasn't as deep as she'd feared at first glance.

"You don't need stitches, but I will bandage this for tonight, to keep the skin in place while it seals. By tomorrow, you should be able to do without the bandages as long as you take it easy." She applied a special salve she had made for such injuries while she spoke, then wound a clean length of bandage around his leg with his assistance.

He lifted his leg enough for her to get underneath. Removing the soaked toweling gave her more room to work, but the cut was high up on his thigh and every trip around the circumference of his thigh brought her in close proximity to his cock. Which was hardening with every revolution of the bandage.

Silla tried not to notice. Some men responded to a healer's touch whether they wanted to or not. Somehow, though, she didn't think Brodie was the kind of man to respond to just any woman's touch. No, the hardness so poorly hidden by his tunic hem and trews was most likely just for her. Especially after that amazing kiss they'd shared in the yard that had left her shaken, stirred and altogether too aroused for her own comfort.

"I would say I was sorry, but I'm not." He must have noticed the direction of her gaze. She felt heat flood her cheeks as her gaze shot to his. He was smiling, but this smile held an ocean of knowledge. A sea of desire.

Dare she dip her toes into the water?

"This sort of thing happens with male patients sometimes." She tried to sound nonchalant, shrugging it off.

"I don't think I like the sound of that." His expression suddenly changed from amused to angry…and possessive? How could he feel possessive of her in so short a time?

"It is a hazard of my profession nonetheless."

He made a sound in between a sigh and a growl that wasn't hard to interpret. Amazingly, he was jealous.

She looked up at him, confused, oddly flattered and—she wasn't too proud to admit—aroused. Again. Still. She wasn't sure which.

Brodie was everything she'd dreamed of in a man and never really thought existed. He was a knight. A man of honor, without doubt. Only honorable men were chosen as knights. Dragons, it was said, were excellent judges of character.

He was also by far the most handsome man she had ever been near. And his attractiveness wasn't just skin-deep. The obvious love he had for his dragon friend showed in his every action. He had been polite, kind, funny and welcoming. Sexy too, though not in a blatant way...until just now. Her eyes were drawn by the erection he did little to hide.

Admittedly, his tunic covered him, just barely. But judging by the impression in the fabric, he could not have easily hid his generous proportions even if he'd tried. Her mouth watered at the thought of touching him. There.

"What is this?" She was baffled by her own reactions. She met his gaze, knowing her flushed face and wide eyes showed her confusion and probably her arousal as well.

"Whatever you want it to be, milady." His voice had turned seductive and low.

On one hand, she wanted him to grab her and take the decision out of her hands, but on the other, she knew he was not the kind of man to force a woman into intimacy—even if she was ultimately willing. No, Silla would have to be bold and make up her own mind. There was no easy way out for her here. She wanted him—a miracle in itself—and yet she was afraid.

"I am not accustomed to this kind of thing." She looked down at her hands, knowing the heat in her cheeks only increased.

Brodie moved, turning so that both of his feet touched the floor and he was left sitting on the side of the bed, next to her. One of his large hands lifted to stroke her cheek, and she found herself leaning into his caress.

"Don't you think I know that? You are a special woman, Silla. I recognized that from almost the first moment we met. I know this is fast, but such is the way with knights."

He shrugged, and she wasn't sure what he meant about knights being faster than others. Perhaps it was the danger of the lifestyle they led? Maybe they seized every moment because they were in such constant danger? The thought made her cringe inwardly. The idea that he put himself in harm's way on a regular basis both frightened her and made her feel pride in him, in his calling.

He leaned closer, but made no move to claim her lips. She could feel the warmth of his breath against her skin, feel the heat of him along her side. She knew what he was doing. He was dangling temptation in her path and seeing if she would take that final step, bridge the small distance between them and take what she wanted. In that way, he would know it truly was what she wanted, not something he had persuaded. Silla was both glad of his care for her feelings and disturbed that she would have to make the move.

Dare she?

Oh, yes, she thought as she joined her lips to his. She most definitely needed to dare this one time. She might come to regret her choice tomorrow, but for tonight, she would live a dream. She would suspend worry and doubt, and share her body with a man too good to be true. Too good to be hers for any longer than the space of a single, stolen night.

She pushed him back down onto the large bed and straddled his hard body. Now that she had made her decision, she had become the aggressor—a role she had never played before but found she enjoyed immensely. She was careful of his wound. It would not do to make him bleed again. Not now, when pleasure was on offer.

She kissed him deeply, plundering and allowing her mouth to be plundered in return. All the while, her fingers were busy with the ties of his tunic, loosening the maddening knots that kept her from her goal—his skin. The more she could touch him, the better.

After a battle with the stubborn fabric, she finally was able to push the tunic up and over his cooperative shoulders. He lifted, helping shift the cloth. Her focus had narrowed to this one man, this huge bed and her desire to join with him in every way she knew how. At least for this one blessed night, never to be repeated.

His chest was heavily muscled and scarred like his legs had been. His arms had taken the worst of the cuts over the years, but though many, few looked as if they had been severe when made. The extent of his injuries distracted her for only a moment, but it was long enough for him to turn the tables.

Brodie rolled, switching places so that she was under him. He'd hiked up the skirt of her simple dress in the process so that it rode around mid-thigh on her. He took quick advantage, planting his knees between hers, using one hand to push the fabric of her dress higher. She wore little beneath, but he was left only in his trews, so she supposed they should be even. Once he rid her of her dress, she would be left with only the thin covering of her pantaloons.

How she wished all the fabric that remained was gone already. She wanted nothing to come between them. Not now. She was too primed. Too ready. She wanted him, inside her, pumping into her waiting, receptive body.

She helped him remove her dress, gasping for air as his hands cupped her bare breasts. She thought she could not want him more. She'd been wrong. As he played with her sensitive nipples, then bent to lick them and suck them into his mouth one at a time, she learned the real meaning of yearning.

A shock of ecstasy made her gasp as pleasure rolled over her in a wave that took her by surprise. He sucked hard on one breast while pinching the other gently in a repetitive motion that made her moan. No man had elicited such responses from her. Not ever.

He pulled back and smiled, and she knew he understood what was going on in her body. His eyes held knowledge that she did not understand and secrets that made him happy for some reason. She didn't question it, she only wanted more of the pleasure he had taught her greedy body. She had become a wanton, it seemed, and all it had taken was this man to bring it about.

"There are still too many clothes," he complained with a smile, nipping at the soft skin of her belly as he stalked lower over her body. His hands untied the little bows of her pantaloons and pulled them down, his mouth following their path with small kisses.

She was shocked when his mouth stopped at the apex of her thighs and the fabric continued its downward slide until it was gone from her body. He spread her legs and then his tongue did the most amazing things to her clit. She'd been taught about anatomy, of course. Every good healer knew the parts of the body and their functions. But never had she fully understood the purpose of the clitoris until now.

Brodie taught her things about her own body that made her want to laugh, cry and scream in pleasure all at the same time. She came again—harder this time, though she would not have believed such a thing was possible—with his mouth on her pussy. Her body hummed and unbelievably, was ready for more when he sat up between her thighs and removed his trews.

And there he was. Magnificent. Large, erect, well-shaped and all for her. At least for tonight. That lovely cock would be the instrument of her pleasure, if the Lady blessed her with yet another new experience.

Silla had been bedded before, but never, it seemed, by such a skilled and caring lover.

So far, this experience had been everything she had dreamed of. Everything she had never thought she would ever experience. Fairy tale stuff about which young women dreamed.

She reached for him, wanting to give him a taste of what he'd already given her, but he stopped her and moved out of range. Her gaze met his and found him smiling gently.

"This time is for you, my dear Silla. It is my time to prove to you what you are capable of. My time to try to convince you this should not be our only time. Maybe tomorrow I'll let you play." He shrugged, though the look in his eyes told her he was looking forward to letting her have her way with him.

"You want more than just this night?" she asked, dumbfounded by his words. Could he really want more than just this? She had not dared hope...

"I want you. Repeatedly. As much as you'll allow and more."

Could he be serious? He looked serious. She began to believe and a small flicker of hope took shape in her heart, a tiny ember that could either be nurtured into flame or left to die on the hearth. Only time would see which way it would go.

"I want you, Brodie. Will you come into me now?" She spoke in a soft voice, slightly embarrassed by the words, but wanting him to know how she felt.

The broadening of his smile was her answer as he moved back between her thighs, positioning himself between her slick folds. His tongue had prepared the way, it seemed, eliciting the response from her body that would allow easy passage for his large size.

She knew the theory of how their parts would fit and had experienced it several times, but never with such a big man and never when she was truly prepared. Never had she responded to any man the way she responded to Brodie.

He slid inside with only minimal difficulty and then just stayed there, filling her. His gaze sought hers and silent communication seemed to pass between them. His eyes asked if she was all right and seemed to find their answer in her expression.

She was more than fine, if truth be told. She was experiencing true desire for the first time in her life and enjoying the feel of him inside her, testing her limits, rubbing against hidden points that made her want to squirm.

It was delightful. And it only got more so when he began to move. A slow rhythm at first that built and built as he watched her every response. A catch in her breath earned her a growl of approval and an increase in the pleasurable assault on her every sense.

His manly scent enticed her. The sound of his grunts and growls made her passion rise higher. The sight of him rising over her, his body straining against hers, was a new dream come true. The feel of him inside her and against her gave her delicious goose bumps and his skin had an almost addictive, salty tang against her mouth.

She felt something monumental gathering inside her. Tension of the most delicious kind and much greater than anything she'd experienced before. Her pleasure increased along with his pace until he was ramming into her in short digs that made her keen on every stroke. She came with a cry wrenched from her soul as he tensed above her, his hot seed flooding her womb with his warmth.

She spoke his name like a prayer as she held on for dear life, her body spinning into the vortex of bliss she had never known. So this then, was what drove so many people.

She thought she finally understood. And it had taken this special man to teach her. Brodie was dear to her. So dear.

She would have said she loved him, if she still believed in such things. But love meant pain in her experience and it never lasted. Still, she was immensely fond of Brodie and would willingly be his bed partner any time he crooked his little finger. She was already addicted to his touch. Addicted to the amazing pleasure only he had ever taken time to show her. Perhaps, she thought, only he could bring it.

A sobering thought.

Brodie withdrew after a long moment and reached over the side of the bed to her stack of clean cloths. Holding her gaze, he wiped between her thighs, cleaning her. It was an intimate act nobody had ever performed for her, and it had the odd effect of making her want him all over again.

Her body was buzzing anew with arousal when he slid his fingers inside her, rubbing up against a spot that made her moan. He captured the sound with his lips as he kissed her senseless.

And that was when she heard another man chuckle.

CHAPTER FIVE

"We fly here in the dead of night because we heard you were injured, and what do I find but your hand up a willing woman's pussy."

"Stars damn your hide, Geoff, you always had lousy timing," Brodie groused, breaking away from Silla's sweet kiss.

He kept her legs splayed and his fingers up her cunt for all to see on purpose, even though she tried to squirm away from him. If she was going to be their wife, she would have to get used to Geoff watching them fuck—and Brodie watching them fuck, for that matter. Better to see if she was up for it now, to avoid misunderstandings.

"This is Silla," Brodie continued. "She is special to me, Geoff, so be polite and I might even see if she's willing to bed you."

"What?" Silla's eyes widened, and Brodie knew he had some fast talking to do.

"Remember when I said marriage in the Lair involved two knights and one woman?" He waited for her to nod, even as he rubbed her clit with slow, deliberate action. "I want you to be my wife, Silla. Mine and Geoff's. Forever. For always. To have and to hold and fuck together and apart." He felt a rush of fluid coat his hands, and he knew the idea appealed. "Think about it, Silla. Two cocks to give you pleasure, two men to cherish you for all your days, two warriors and their dragon partners to protect you always, and two hearts to share your love."

"Are you serious?" Silla's words were breathed in a whisper so low he hardly heard it. But the renewed thrum of her body under his gave him hope.

"As serious as I have ever been in my life. Knights often know right away when they meet the woman who is meant to share their lives. It is a blessing of our kind. I knew earlier this evening that I had met my match. Geoff's too, though you don't know him yet. I would bet everything I hold dear that once you get to know him a little, he will feel about you the way I already do."

"What way is that?" Her breath caught as he increased the pressure of his fingers inside her channel. He lowered his head to kiss her nipple, drawing it to a peak that made her gasp before he answered.

"I believe I will love you, Silla." He phrased his declaration carefully, guessing from the description of her past that she was cynical about love, and had no belief in love at first sight. "Now please let me fuck you again before I explode, then we can sit down with Geoff and you can get to know him a little." He didn't wait for her reply, turning to Geoff and jerking his head toward the chair near the bed. "Sit down and be quiet. This won't take but a moment."

"You want him to watch?" she asked in a shocked whisper as Brodie settled between her legs once more.

He wasn't about to chance her leaving if he let her up even for a second. She needed to come again and again until she was used to his touch and addicted to the pleasure he could give her. This was also a test of sorts. Dragons were notorious exhibitionists. When the dragons took to the sky in their mating flights, they didn't always check to see that their human counterparts were in a private place first. Lair life was lusty, and unmated knights often ended up being voyeurs to some extent. It was accepted as a matter of necessity when living with dragons.

Would Silla be open to the experience? And would she be able to share herself with Geoff as she had done with Brodie? This was the first step to finding out.

Brodie removed his fingers and slid his cock into her without much fuss. He was sure to spread her legs wide so Geoff could see as much as possible. He played with Silla's generous breasts as he pumped within her, mindful of the audience, which excited the inner exhibitionist all knights seemed to carry.

He noted the direction of her gaze. Several times she looked over at Geoff, blushing to the roots of her hair but excited all the same. For it was at those times when she met Geoff's very interested gaze that her body gave forth its nectar around his cock, lubricating his way. Oh yes, she was interested. She was responding very well to this little unplanned test.

Brodie slowed his pace, wanting to push her closer to her limits. He pulled her thighs over his and leaned back, cupping her breasts in his hands.

"Our Silla has lovely round tits, doesn't

she, Geoff?"

"What in the hells are you doing?" Geoff asked in the privacy of their minds. It was a gift of their partnering with dragons that they could communicate silently with each other as well. *"You're going to scare her off. If she really is the one for us, we have to be careful how we handle her."*

"Oh, she is our mate, Geoff. I have little doubt of that. She can hear Phelan."

"Truly?" Geoff's tone held hope. *"She can bespeak dragons?"*

"Truly, brother. She can. She is our mate. It is time we taught her what that means."

Geoff stood and came over to the bedside. They were in the middle of the huge mattress, so there was room for the other knight to sit.

Geoff reached out and plucked at the nipple standing upright on the closest breast. Brodie still cupped her, but Geoff tugged at her nipple, working together as they would for the rest of their lives—if Silla agreed.

"Very fine indeed," Geoff agreed. "But does she follow orders?"

"And you said I was pushing things? You really want to try your discipline games on her now?" Brodie complained to his fighting partner,

who he knew occasionally liked a bit of kink from his bed sport.

"Why not? If she is the one for us, she will be excited by the idea, don't you think?"

"If this goes badly, I will never forgive you."

Geoff seemed to rethink his plan and bent to retrieve some of Silla's bandages. She'd left her satchel open wide so she could easily access things and Geoff was taking full advantage.

"Does milady allow you to command her pleasure?" Geoff asked aloud. "Does she trust you enough to let me tie her to the bedpost?"

Silla's body jumped under him and Brodie tried to read her expression. He bent, placing his lips next to her ear.

"Geoff is friskier than I, I'm afraid. He likes to play games, but he will not harm you in any way, my love. Nor will I. I promise you on my life. My word as a knight. Do you trust me? I will guide you and protect you, but you must trust me or we will not go any further."

"What are you planning to do to me?" The question came out frightened, but Brodie could hear the small quiver of arousal in her tone as well. And the way her sweet cunny clenched repeatedly around his cock told him she was excited rather than truly scared.

He kissed her cheek, nibbling on her earlobe. "I plan to love you and bring you the greatest pleasure you've ever known. Again and again. But only if you trust me. I will not let you come to harm. What say you?" He had to have her answer before he let this go any further. She was too important to him—to all of them.

"I consent, but if I ask you to stop, you must promise me that you will."

"I vow it." He kissed her again, loving the way she clenched around him. "Now, raise your arms. We are going to tie you up."

Geoff took the arm closest to him and quickly looped a bit of the soft bandage around her wrist, tying the other end to the headboard. Brodie did the same on the other side. He had to leave the warm heat of her pussy to do it, but they had time now. She wasn't going to bolt. At least not until she called a halt and they untied her. He had time to entice her, to explore her, to ravish her slowly.

Time to introduce Geoff into the play, in small increments. As much as she could handle, or would allow. The sooner the three of them got used to each other, the sooner they could cement the bonds to join their little family and the dragons could mate. Silla would be the link that held them all together. If they did this right. And if she agreed to be their wife.

A lot was riding on the next few hours.

CHAPTER SIX

Silla didn't know why she wasn't running for the hills. A strange man was tying her naked to a giant bed, and she was letting him! What had changed about her sanity in the past hour that she would allow such a thing?

But the little devil of lust that had finally been awakened in her body was driving her to comply with anything Brodie and his fighting partner asked. She'd heard about the threesomes in the Lairs around the country and always wondered how that might work. Here was her golden opportunity to find out. And most shocking of all, Brodie even said he wanted her to be their wife.

She still couldn't quite believe that part. She had been a wife and never thought she would ever contemplate such a thing again, but she had never dreamed a knight—make that *two* knights—would want her for their mate. She didn't know what to think about that. But she definitely wanted to know more of the pleasure that Brodie had introduced her to.

She couldn't deny that Geoff's gaze fired her senses. Perhaps she had hidden exhibitionist tendencies after all. She never would have believed it, but when Geoff had stared at her pussy while Brodie had been inside her, the intent expression on his face had made her breathless. And when they'd both touched her breast at the same time, she'd felt greedy for more.

Brodie alone had been incredible, but the forbidden allure of having two men touch her at the same time was fast becoming irresistible. Could she actually be contemplating allowing the newcomer to not only touch her, but to take her as well? Something she wouldn't even have considered only an hour ago was easily becoming the most tantalizing thought imaginable.

How would it work? What would it feel like? Would she survive such a thing and would they still want her after they'd gotten a taste of her?

All questions she would soon know the

answer to, if she let this continue.

When her hands were secure, they shocked her by moving to her feet. One on each side. Spreading her legs and tying her ankles to the rail at the bottom of the wide bed. There was quite a bit of give in the long bandages they'd used to tie her, so she could move a little. She could bend her elbows and, more importantly, her knees. She imagined all sorts of scenarios that required bent knees and just the carnal thoughts in her mind made her temperature rise higher.

When she was spread-eagled before them, Brodie sat naked on one side of her, Geoff fully clothed on the other.

Geoff held her gaze as he began to remove his leather jerkin. Lace by lace, she watched him untie the leather that protected him while in flight with his dragon partner.

Geoff had blond hair and bright blue eyes. He was a perfect foil to Brodie's brown-haired, brown-eyed handsomeness. Geoff was more rugged-looking, while Brodie was prettier, but both were built on the massive side, with bulging muscles and the scars of the warrior life. Geoff shrugged out of his leather jerkin and yanked the cloth tunic he wore under it over his head.

She was a little breathless as she got her first look at his well-formed chest and arms. He had fewer scars than Brodie, but that was probably because, as Brodie had told her, he was younger. Of course, they both looked about the same age—slightly younger than her, even though they were older in years and mileage, if their scars were anything to go by.

Geoff held her gaze as his fingers trailed down the skin of her abdomen and back up again to tease lightly around her breast, drawing circles. He then transferred his attention to what his hand was doing, observing her body as if he were looking at a sculpture or a piece of fine art. He played with her nipple until it stood upright, as if begging for his touch.

"When you are tied up for our pleasure, you will address us as Sir. Is that clear?"

His words took her by surprise, and she hesitated. Geoff pinched her nipple, making her squeak, though it didn't hurt so much as shock her.

"I said, is that clear?" he repeated, waiting for an answer, his fingers rolling her nipple, soothing and exciting all at once.

"Yes," she gasped.

He pinched her again. Harder this time.

"Yes, what?"

It took her a moment to focus as he returned to rolling her pointed nipple between his thumb and forefinger.

"Yes, Sir?"

He let go and moved his hand back. "Very good. Kiss it better, Brodie. She seems to like your mouth on her tits."

Brodie moved into her line of vision and smiled at her before sucking her breast into his warm mouth. He used his tongue on her, eliciting a moan of pleasure from her throat.

"Ah, yes, she does like you, Brodie." Geoff's voice claimed her attention, as did the hand that started a path from her navel down to the apex of her spread thighs. Geoff's light touch circled around her clit, sliding through the fluid that came forth at his touch, and she saw the smile on his face, though he didn't meet her gaze. He was staring intently downward and she realized he was studying her crotch.

Her face flamed. Nobody had ever given her such an intent inspection in that area. It wasn't seemly. Yet, it aroused her a great deal. More than she would have ever credited.

Geoff moved downward while Brodie still applied himself to her breasts, and she felt Geoff's hands gently bending her knees and separating her thighs as far as they would go. He had full access now and he wasn't long in using it. Both of his hands went to her pussy, spreading the lips apart while his face drew close enough that she could feel the waft of his warm breath over her most sensitive skin.

He kept her spread while one finger teased her clit and then, without warning, he let go and one long finger plunged into her channel, sliding right up into her core. Hard, fast and unexpected. Combined with the way Brodie was licking and sucking on her breasts, she felt sensation wash over her in a wave of completion. A small completion, now that she knew what Brodie could bring her if he really tried, but completion nonetheless.

Geoff withdrew his finger and patted her curls.

"Good girl," he said softly, his face coming back into view.

He still wore his leather pants, and the sight of him kneeling near her head brought her back to full arousal. To have two such handsome men focused solely on her body—on her pleasure—was a truly amazing thing.

"Have you sucked Brodie's cock yet?" he asked unexpectedly.

"No...Sir." She remembered his rules just in time.

"No? I thought for certain he would have stuck it down your throat already." The crude expression added something naughty, in a good way, to the proceedings, oddly enough.

Brodie moved away from her breasts and sat at her side, reaching up to hold the fingers of one hand, as if reassuring her.

"We haven't had a lot of time together, Geoff." Brodie's voice sounded like a warning, and she knew he was looking out for her comfort.

"No matter. It is easily rectified." Geoff lowered his face so his lips rested next to Silla's ear and he spoke in a low voice, his breath puffing against the shell of her ear with every word. "I know you do not know me yet, but if we are meant to be a family, we will learn each other in time. The question is, will you let me fuck you tonight? I allow you to decide, Lady Silla. Will you suck Brodie's cock while I learn the heat of your core? Or will you suck me while Brodie reclaims what he has known once already? Or will I stand aside and allow Brodie to bring you to completion? Simply tell me what you desire and this you shall have."

Goddess, what temptation! Silla didn't know where these desires were coming from and didn't care to question. The touch of these two men had driven her to a place of desperation, a place of yearning, a place of need. She wanted it all. And even if it was just for tonight, she wanted them both. Let the morning take care of itself. Tonight she wanted the dream. The fantasy. The ecstasy.

Geoff waited, his face very close to hers. He lifted slightly, his gaze meeting and holding hers.

"What is it to be, milady?"

For the first time, she saw the vulnerability in his eyes. She understood a little bit more about this strange knight and knew she could deny him nothing in this moment. Tomorrow might be another story, but for now, she was his. His and Brodie's.

"The first thing, Sir," she found the nerve to answer in the barest whisper. She saw the fire leap in his eyes as her words found their mark.

Geoff lowered his lips to hers in their first kiss. A gentle kiss of reverence. A tender salute that turned molten as his tongue met and dueled with hers. She didn't know how long it lasted, but when he lifted his head, the room was spinning. She was dizzy with desire and drunk on him.

"You will never regret this, my dear. I vow it."

Geoff moved up to kneel at her side, his fingers working on the fly of his leather pants. He pulled them down, freeing an impressive erection, holding her gaze all the while. She wanted to lick him, to learn his taste, but he moved away, down to where her thighs were still spread wide apart.

She was surprised when his hands sought the ties that held her ankles, freeing her. Brodie freed her wrists as well and together they coaxed her to turn over onto her hands and knees.

The new position brought her head in alignment with Brodie's straining cock and suddenly, she wanted to learn its texture and taste against her tongue. She didn't give him warning, simply licking her way up his cock while he was distracted watching Geoff prepare her.

Geoff's hands spread her thighs and his fingers speared into her, drawing out her moisture while she sucked Brodie's cock deep into her mouth. He tasted salty and divine, while Geoff kept her off balance with the thrust of his fingers. They left and were soon replaced by his cock.

He slid in slowly, the curve of his long hardness making the feel of him somewhat different from Brodie. He pushed in and she realized his rhythm against her backside drove her deeper onto Brodie in front.

She liked it. The rhythm he set up pleased them all and before long they were grunting, groaning and straining against each other in an ever-increasing pace. When Geoff slapped her ass, she squeaked in surprise. It felt oddly good as she clenched on him, and he did it again, eliciting the same response. She couldn't take much of such treatment. It was too exciting. Too different and foreign to anything she'd experienced before.

She came in a rush and would have screamed if not for the cock in her mouth. Brodie came a moment later, pulling out of her mouth to shoot his come over her hanging breasts. She rose up slightly and pressed her breasts against him, prolonging the moment for them both. Geoff was still pumping within her when Brodie drew away, collapsing against the headboard, watching them.

Geoff's arms snaked around her and cupped her breasts, sliding in the come left there by Brodie, rubbing repeatedly over her nipples in a way that made her want to scream. Her climax extended, becoming two and then three orgasms while he continued to pound into her from behind.

When he tensed and squeezed her nipples hardest of all, she exploded one last time and felt the warmth of his come inside her, sliding, slipping and dripping as he continued to pulse in and out of her core. She did scream then, an incoherent sound of the most amazing pleasure she'd ever known. Made all the more alluring by the heated brown gaze of Brodie, watching them.

Dammit. Maybe she really was an exhibitionist after all.

CHAPTER SEVEN

They made love all night long, singly and in triad, and finally found sleep a few hours before dawn. Silla woke as the first beams of light came in through the window, knowing she had to see to her patient. She slid out of the bed as quietly as possible. The knights had taken up positions on either side of her and did not stir as she dressed and slipped out into the early morning light.

She found two dragons where there had been only one the night before. They lay very close, their necks entwined. She paused to watch them for a moment. They looked so happy…

She saw now, in the morning light, that Phelan was a metallic bronze in color, while the female who lay close to him was so deep a blue, she was almost purple. Their colors were complementary and the shine of their scales was something she had not expected. Instead of leathery, they looked almost like polished metal. Yet they were supple and able to bend in ways she had not expected of creatures so large.

"Good morrow, Lady Silla," came the rumbly voice she'd heard last night inside her mind. Phelan was speaking to her, and she finally noticed his eyes blinking open.

"Good morrow, Sir Phelan. How do you feel today?" she asked aloud, not sure how to—or even if she could—reply the same way.

"I am well and happy. My mate is here and our knights report that we may soon be together again." The other dragon stirred and opened her eyes. They unwound their long necks and both giant heads rose a few feet in the air to stare down at her.

As they moved, she noted the almost iridescent sheen of their scales as the light played off them. The dragon, who had been impressive in the lantern lit night, was almost overwhelming in the light of day. She wondered how magnificent he would appear when the sun's rays grew stronger and kissed his living armor.

"May I approach? Sir Brodie and I

prepared more burnjelly last night that will make you more comfortable this morning, I believe." She held the bowls in her hands aloft for the dragon to see.

"Thank you for your care of my mate," came another voice in her mind. This one was somehow softer, though no less immense. It was the female dragon, speaking directly to her for the first time. *"I am Qwila."*

"I am Silla," she replied, cracking an involuntary smile when she realized their names rhymed. She saw the dragons chuckle as tendrils of cinnamon-scented smoke rose into the early morning air.

"It was my honor," she went on. "I am a journeyman healer of the High Temple of Our Lady of Light. Though I have never treated a dragon before, I am sworn to provide care to all of Her creatures, human and otherwise."

"We know of your Order," Phelan answered. *"Osric is a part of our extended family through Brodie. Osric would have made an excellent knight, if not for his penchant to heal things rather than demolish them."*

Again came the little spirals of smoke that indicated dragonish amusement. Silla found herself smiling as well. Phelan had summed up Osric's nature perfectly. A gentler man she had never met. It would be impossible for him to wield a sword, even in defense of innocents. He was a pacifist through and through.

"Your skills will be an excellent addition to our new Lair. We have no healer yet and would be hard pressed to find one of your skill willing to live and work with our kind," Qwila added. *"Believe it or not, many people are afraid of us."* Her tone indicated wry humor that Silla appreciated. Dragons really weren't scary at all, once you were able to speak to them a bit.

But Qwila was talking as if Silla's joining their little group was already set in stone. Silla still had doubts.

"May I?" she reminded the dragons, proffering the burnjelly bowls again.

"Yes, please," Phelan answered in her mind. He moved his wing slightly, so she could get as close as possible to the worst of his wounds. Qwila helped, using her own wing to prop his up and take some of the weight off the joint that had been damaged.

Phelan lowered his head to the ground, resting it on his forearms and closing his eyes. Qwila's head rose over Silla's, watching intently as she examined the wound.

"This has done better than I expected," Silla reported as she inspected the deep red gash that had begun to heal at record pace. "If it is not too painful for you, I will apply the burnjelly directly. It should make you feel much more comfortable as soon as it begins to absorb."

"Thank you, healer. I will let you know if I cannot bear the agony." Phelan's voice held a teasing note, and she realized she was treating him as she would her human patients. Undoubtedly the dragon's tolerances were quite different indeed.

"Forgive me, Sir Phelan. I see I have much to learn about your kind." She saw the amused smoke rising from his nostrils a few yards away and was amazed again at his sense of humor.

"Not to worry," Qwila's voice rumbled through her mind. *"You will have many decades to perfect your knowledge of how to treat our kind once you formally join your life to our knights, and by their connection, to us."*

Silla's hands paused, then continued in their work. Phelan's wound required all the burnjelly they'd prepared and probably could have taken more, but she'd have to raid more of her plants in order to get it.

"I'm still not sure about all of this." She decided to be candid with the dragons, since they seemed to be under the impression she really was going to marry their knights. "I dare not believe it's real."

"It is as real as I am." Qwila's head lowered so she could look into Silla's eyes. The dragon seemed completely serious. *"You are the woman the Mother of All has chosen for our knights. For our family. You can hear us!"* She seemed particularly impressed by that fact. *"Do you know how rare that is?"*

"Um…no. Is it?" Silla felt unsure.

"Rarer than diamonds, my dear doubter," Phelan piped in, his head still reclining on his forelegs and his eyes still closed. *"We know you are the one. Our knights know it. It is only for you to understand and agree."*

"You make it sound so simple." Finished with her work on his wound, she stepped back so she could see both of the dragons at once while they continued their conversation.

"It is simple. Search your heart," Qwila advised. *"You know that deep down, you are already joined to them both. It is only for you to accept the connection and allow it to open wider so that it will never be closed. Through your bond to our*

knights, you will connect with us as well and our magic will sustain you for many, many years."

"It seems incredible," Silla whispered, dropping her gaze. She felt at sea, lost to all the change that had come to her life in such a short time.

"It's real," Brodie's voice came to her from behind as he moved in and tugged her back against him. His arms held her, making her feel safe in the sea of confusion that had surrounded her in the past hours since arriving in Bayberry Heath.

He kissed her temple, his arms around her waist. "I feel more in my heart for you, Silla, than I ever have for any other woman. Knights know their mate almost immediately. You are mine. And Geoff's. The fact that you can talk to these two only confirms it." Humor laced his tone as he referred to the dragons. "If you give us a chance, we will convince you that you truly belong with us for all time. As you know, we can be very persuasive." He turned her in his arms and the joy she found in his expression was enchanting.

Geoff walked up as Brodie let her go, and saying nothing, he took her into his arms, rocking her gently from side to side as he hugged her. Enfolding her in his tallness, his power, his strength. Far from being overwhelmed, she found she loved the sensation.

Almost as much as she loved him? Could she really love him—and Brodie—in so short an acquaintance?

Geoff's hug changed as he drew back and lowered his face to match his lips to hers in a sweet, gentle, unexpected kiss. When he drew back, she saw an unaccountable brightness in his eyes, as if he was almost overcome with emotion.

"I pushed you far last night. I did not believe love at first sight was real, even though many tales speak of such things between knights and their mates. Forgive me? I am convinced beyond the shadow of a doubt that you are the missing piece to our family. With you—and only you, dear Silla—can we all be happy. Will you do that for us? Will you make us the happiest of men, and allow our dragon partners to be together once more?"

"But what of my work?" She asked the first thing that popped into her mind. She didn't know what to say. The wild part of her heart wanted to jump into their arms and never look back, but her practical side was casting doubts. She had never been lucky in marriage before. She had resigned herself to living a life of service and solitude. Why should things change so drastically for her now?

Geoff smiled. "Your skills will be much in demand in the Lair. In fact, we will be lucky to see you at all once everyone knows you are a Temple-trained healer. Such things are rare in the outlying Lairs."

"And what about Hero? What's to become of him?"

"Hero? Who is that?" Geoff asked, clearly puzzled.

"My horse." But the old gelding was more than that. He was her friend, confidant, and had been her constant companion these past few years. She didn't want to leave him to the care of strangers.

"You named that old nag Hero?" Brodie chuckled from the side.

"He's not a nag. He's my friend, and I won't leave him behind."

"You won't have to, my love," Geoff assured her with a little squeeze. "He will have oats and hay and a warm place to live out his life. There is a stable built into the

Lair for the beasts of burden we use to cart supplies. He will live there and you can see him every day."

"And my brother, Osric, will make things right with the Temple," Brodie put in, moving closer. Geoff stepped to her right to allow Brodie room on her left. They both took one of her hands. Geoff kept his arm around her shoulder, while Brodie looped one loosely around her waist. "The Temple's loss will be our gain. And if we haven't said it before, be assured Geoff and I will never harm you. We will never stray from you. You will be our touchstone and our guiding light. You are the woman we have been searching for. Only you, Silla, until the Mother calls us all home to Her Light."

Tears filled Silla's eyes as his words calmed her fears and made her hope. Did she dare trust these men? These knights of the realm?

Everyone knew there were no better men in the realm of Draconia than the noble knights who were chosen for their honor as much as their skill by magical dragons who could see into their very soul. Why did she doubt, when both Brodie and Geoff had already proven their worth simply by being chosen as knights?

They would not hurt her. They would not scorn her. They would never throw her out into the street. And everyone knew there was no such thing as divorce among knights and their mates.

Her fears laid to rest, Silla did the only thing she could do. She kissed each of her knights on the cheek and whispered the word that all four beings waited to hear.

"Yes."

#

NOTE FROM BIANCA D'ARC

Thanks for reading *The Dragon Healer (Dragon Knights #5)*. If you enjoyed this book, please consider leaving a review. The next book in the series is the second of three novellas *Master at Arms*.

I just wanted to make note of the various print editions in which this story has appeared. In 2012, my publisher at the time, decided to reissue all of the older ***Dragon Knights*** books with new cover art. For the new editions, they wanted to separate the first two books (which had previously been combined into a single print edition) into two standalone editions, but they also asked that I write two prequel novellas to include as bonus material in the new editions.

As a result, *The Dragon Healer* and *Master at Arms* were written, but never quite made a comfortable fit into the beginning of the series. We tried to label them as Books 1.5 and 2.5, but each vendor had their own rules for how to designate volume numbers within series and it never quite worked. Needless to say, this has caused a great deal of confusion for readers.

When the rights reverted to Hawk Publishing, LLC, in early 2017, we resolved to reissue all the ebooks first, then try to clarify the reading order and reissue everything in print that would have a corresponding ebook, so as to alleviate some of the confusion surrounding this series.

We also purchased the cover art from the 2013 editions of the books, to keep a little bit of continuity. So, what you have here is the first stand-alone edition of ***The Dragon Healer***. The cover art, however, was first used on the stand-alone ebook release of this story in 2013.

In order to rationalize the numbering and reading order information, we're going to be using the following scheme:

1. Maiden Flight
2. Border Lair
3. The Ice Dragon
4. Prince of Spies

These first four were originally known

collectively as the *Daughters of the Dragon* set of books, and always belonged together because they are the story of Adora, Belora, Lana and Riki – a mother and her three daughters.

Then, in the original order of the books, before the first reissues, there was a breakaway novella that took the series in a slightly different direction. I now believe the two other novellas that were written for the first rerelease probably belong with this other one. So, the next set of novellas would be:

5. The Dragon Healer
6. Master at Arms
7. Wings of Change

The next set of novels deal mostly with the men of the royal family and their advisors and used to be known as the *Sons of Draconia* set of books. They are:

8. FireDrake
9. Dragon Storm
10. Keeper of the Flame
11. Hidden Dragons

Then we come to the first trilogy in the series. This set of three full-length novels tells the complex story of just five characters and is known as *The Sea Captain's Daughter* trilogy:

12. Sea Dragon
13. Dragon Fire
14. Dragon Mates

As of this printing, that's where the series stands. There will be more books, starting in 2018, that continue the overall story arc until we resolve the final battle for the Citadel.

Thanks for reading and I hope you continue to enjoy the books!

ABOUT THE AUTHOR

Bianca D'Arc has run a laboratory, climbed the corporate ladder in the shark-infested streets of lower Manhattan, studied and taught martial arts, and earned the right to put a whole bunch of letters after her name, but she's always enjoyed writing more than any of her other pursuits. She grew up and still lives on Long Island, where she keeps busy with an extensive garden, several aquariums full of very demanding fish, and writing her favorite genres of paranormal, fantasy and sci-fi romance.

Bianca loves to hear from readers and can be reached through Twitter (@BiancaDArc), Facebook (BiancaDArcAuthor) or through the various links on her website.

WELCOME TO THE D'ARC SIDE…
WWW.BIANCADARC.COM

OTHER BOOKS BY BIANCA D'ARC

Paranormal Romance

Brotherhood of Blood
One & Only
Rare Vintage
Phantom Desires
Sweeter Than Wine
Forever Valentine
Wolf Hills*
Wolf Quest

Tales of the Were
Lords of the Were
Inferno

Tales of the Were ~ The Others
Rocky
Slade

Tales of the Were ~ Redstone Clan
The Purrfect Stranger
Grif
Red
Magnus
Bobcat
Matt

Tales of the Were ~ String of Fate
Cat's Cradle
King's Throne
Jacob's Ladder
Her Warriors

Tales of the Were ~ Grizzly Cove
All About the Bear
Mating Dance
Night Shift
Alpha Bear
Saving Grace
Bearliest Catch
The Bear's Healing Touch
The Luck of the Shifters
Badass Bear

Tales of the Were ~
Were-Fey Love Story
Lone Wolf
Snow Magic
Midnight Kiss

Tales of the Were ~
Jaguar Island (Howls)
The Jaguar Tycoon
The Jaguar Bodyguard

Gemini Project
Tag Team
Doubling Down

Guardians of the Dark
Half Past Dead
Once Bitten, Twice Dead
A Darker Shade of Dead
The Beast Within
Dead Alert

Gifts of the Ancients: Warrior's Heart

Epic Fantasy Erotic Romance

Dragon Knights

Daughters of the Dragon
Maiden Flight*
Border Lair
The Ice Dragon**
Prince of Spies***

Dragon Knights ~ Novellas
The Dragon Healer
Master at Arms
Wings of Change

Sons of Draconia
FireDrake
Dragon Storm
Keeper of the Flame
Hidden Dragons

The Sea Captain's Daughter
Sea Dragon
Dragon Fire
Dragon Mates

Science Fiction Romance

StarLords
Hidden Talent
Talent For Trouble
Shy Talent

Jit'Suku Chronicles ~ Arcana
King of Swords
King of Cups
King of Clubs
King of Stars
End of the Line

Jit'Suku Chronicles ~ Sons of Amber
Angel in the Badlands

Futuristic Erotic Romance

Resonance Mates
Hara's Legacy**
Davin's Quest
Jaci's Experiment
Grady's Awakening
Harry's Sacrifice

* RT Book Reviews Awards Nominee
** EPPIE Award Winner
*** CAPA Award Winner

DRAGON KNIGHTS 6
THE NOVELLAS 2
MASTER AT ARMS

One dragon to play matchmaker…two knights to serve a lady's every pleasure.

When the call to arms goes out, the dragon Golgorath is the first to take to the skies. Until he finds a knight to equal his heart and fighting skill, Rath flies alone while his mate must wait for her knight, Thorn, to climb on her back. The battleground is a familiar one, an old keep, a noble house without a patriarch, under attack from the evil, snake-like skiths.

Lady Cara can fight, but knows better than to try

to lead men. With her brother wounded, she relies on her new Master at Arms, Tristan. He is a mysterious, recklessly brave foreigner who can never be hers, as she is to be married off to the highest bidder.

Amidst the battle, Rath spies the warrior doing the impossible—slaying a skith single-handed. Rath realizes fate may have just stepped in to help both dragons and men. In Tristan, Rath sees a man worthy of being his knight and, together with Thorn, win Lady Cara's heart into a triad of love. If Tristan's loyalties can first be won by dragonkind.

Note: When two dragons really want something, it's best not to stand in their way. And when their knights are focused on a single woman, nothing and no one will stop them from getting what they want. Beware! This trio gets up to all kinds of naughtiness in the pursuit of true love.

WWW.BIANCADARC.COM